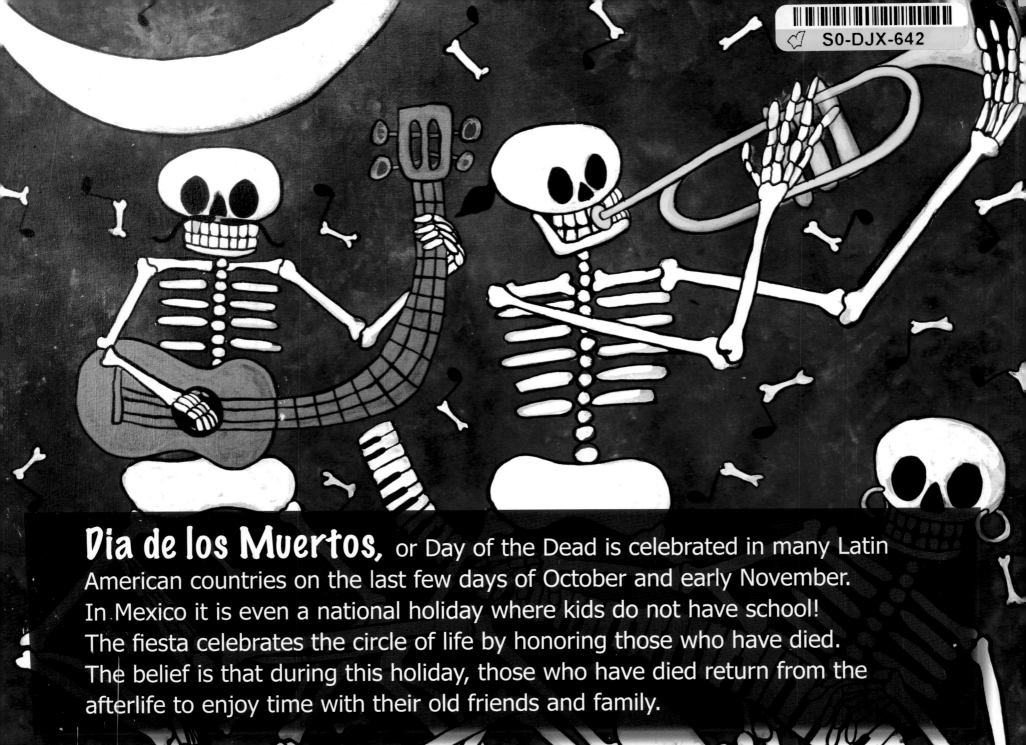

Dia de los Muertos, or Day of the Dead is celebrated in many Latin American countries on the last few days of October and early November. In Mexico it is even a national holiday where kids do not have school! The fiesta celebrates the circle of life by honoring those who have died. The belief is that during this holiday, those who have died return from the afterlife to enjoy time with their old friends and family.

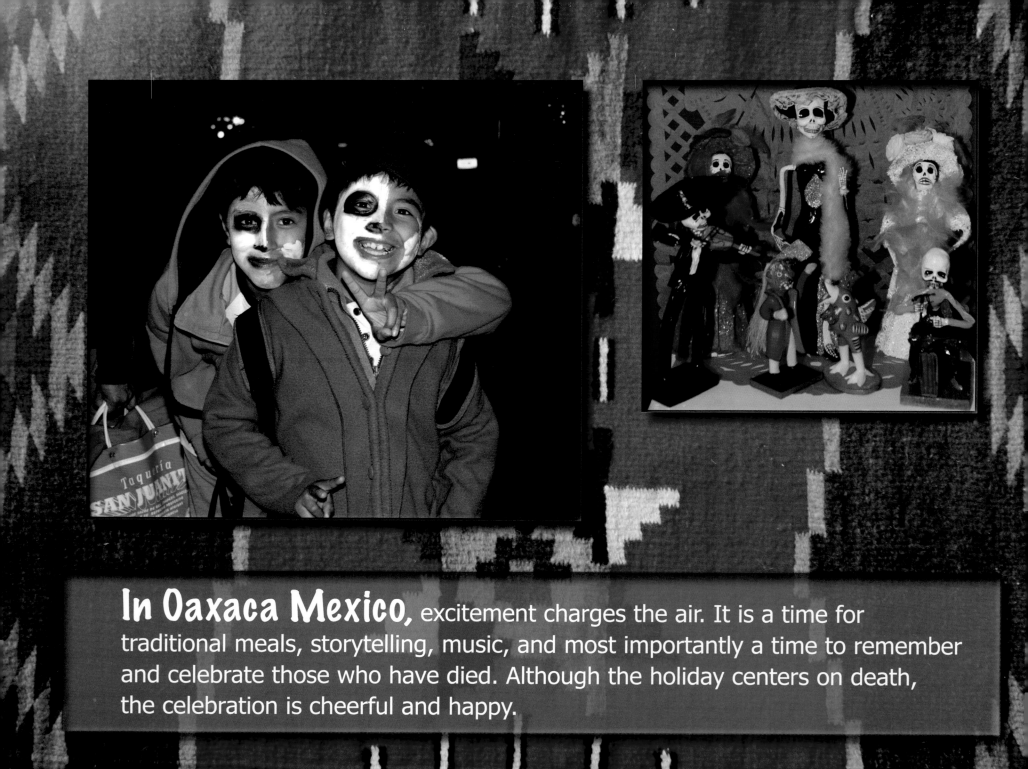

In Oaxaca Mexico, excitement charges the air. It is a time for traditional meals, storytelling, music, and most importantly a time to remember and celebrate those who have died. Although the holiday centers on death, the celebration is cheerful and happy.

Sand paintings are completed in the **_zocolo_**. Children spend hours thinking about their costumes for the fiesta and helping family members shop and decorate for the festive gatherings. The cemeteries are filled with beautiful flowers and generations of family members.

From community to community and home to home, some activities are common to everyone. The preparation of the **altar de los muertos**, cleaning and decorating the gravesites,

visits to the cemetery, and spending time with family are examples of these common activities. Children and adults also dress in fabulous costumes and participate in the **comparsa**.

Building an Altar

is a way to honor the life of ancestors. The *altar de los muertos* is built in tiers and is decorated with flowers, candles, *papel picado*, fruit, *pan de los muertos*, chocolate, *calaveritas de azucar*, and favorite foods of the person who has died. A glass of water may be added to quench the thirst of the spirits.

Families build *altar de los muertos* in their homes. The altars are also displayed in schools, restaurants, stores, community buildings, and businesses.

Preparing the gravestone

for the Day of the Dead is another important activity. Pulling weeds, sweeping away leaves, and decorating with flowers and candles are projects which involve family members of all ages. It is a wonderful time when entire communities join together to celebrate the lives of those who have died.

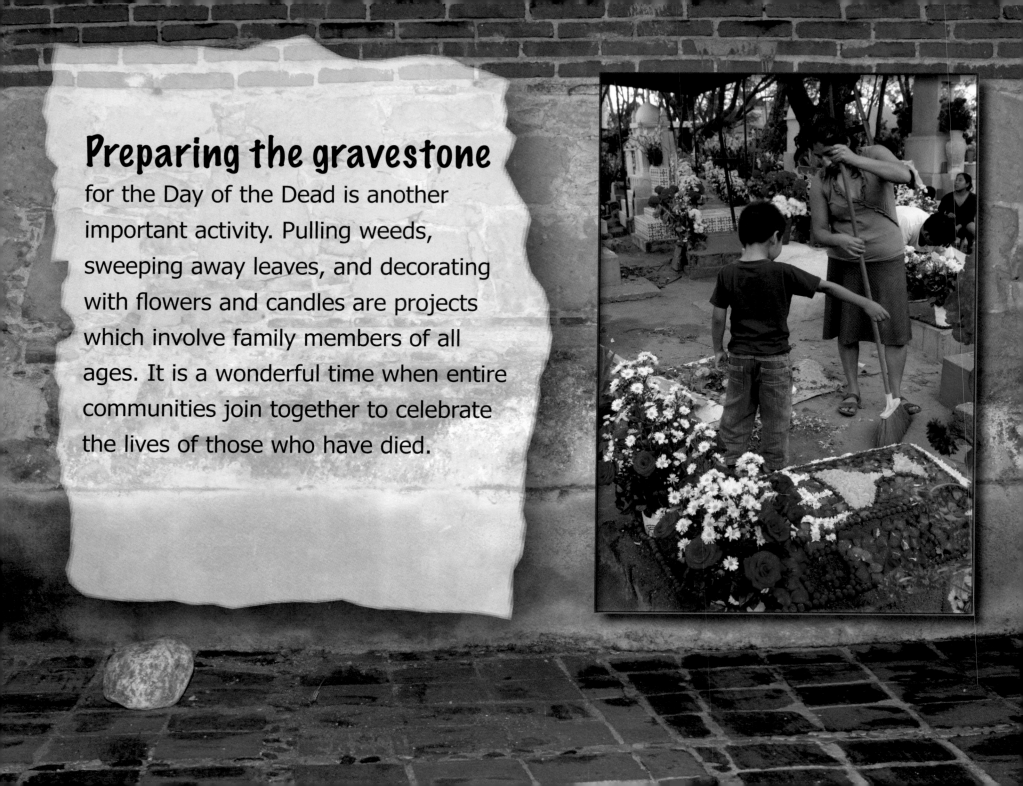

At the weekly markets, almost anything can be found. Meat hangs on hooks from long metal poles. Brightly colored flowers are carried home in large bundles. There are even bowls of fried grasshoppers and live worms for sale!

Products such as fruits and vegetables are grown locally and brought to the market by the farmers. Traditional Day of the Dead items such as *cempazuchitl, copal*, and *mole* are available in the market.

Mounds of **pan de los muertos**, different colored chilies, and live chickens and turkeys are purchased at the market and taken home for the holiday meals.

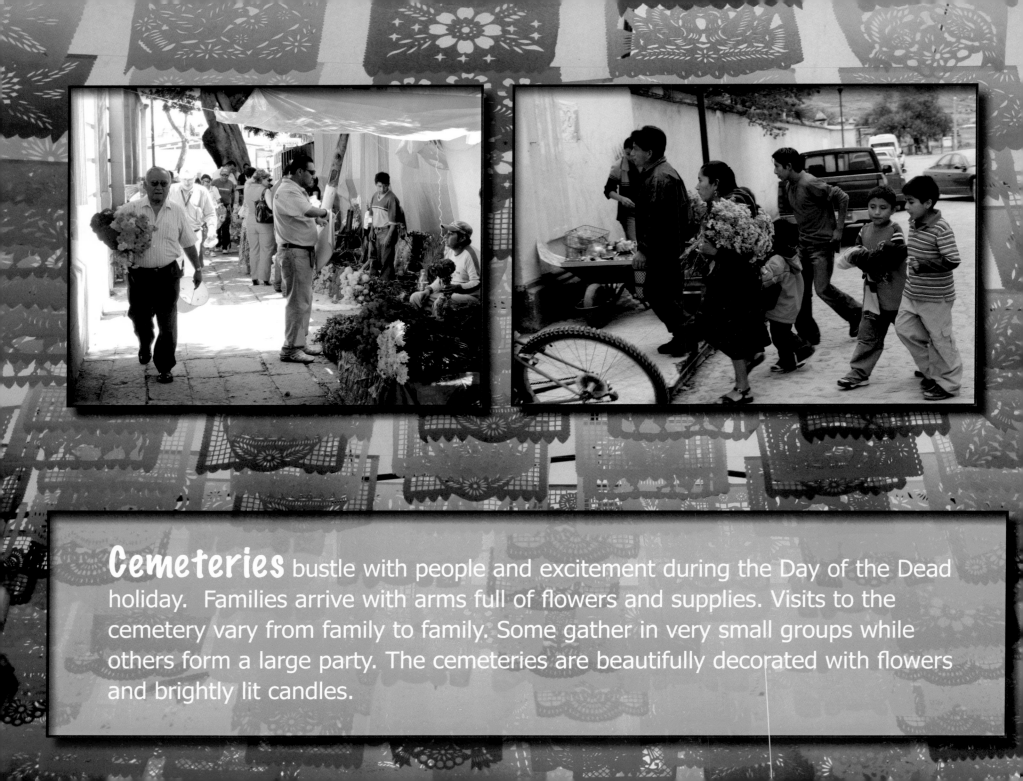

Cemeteries bustle with people and excitement during the Day of the Dead holiday. Families arrive with arms full of flowers and supplies. Visits to the cemetery vary from family to family. Some gather in very small groups while others form a large party. The cemeteries are beautifully decorated with flowers and brightly lit candles.

The cemetery is bursting with color, and the scent of calla lilies, marigolds, cockscomb, and *copal* fills the air.

Lively music from small bands and strolling musicians blends with the chatter of families and friends, and can be heard throughout the cemeteries late into the night.

Families feel the strong presence of their loved ones' souls who return from the afterlife to be with them.

During this special time families pass on stories and lovingly remember those who have died. Some families spend the entire night at the cemetery, only leaving when the sun comes up.

For a few days every fall, the cemeteries
in Mexico are a center of activity and life.

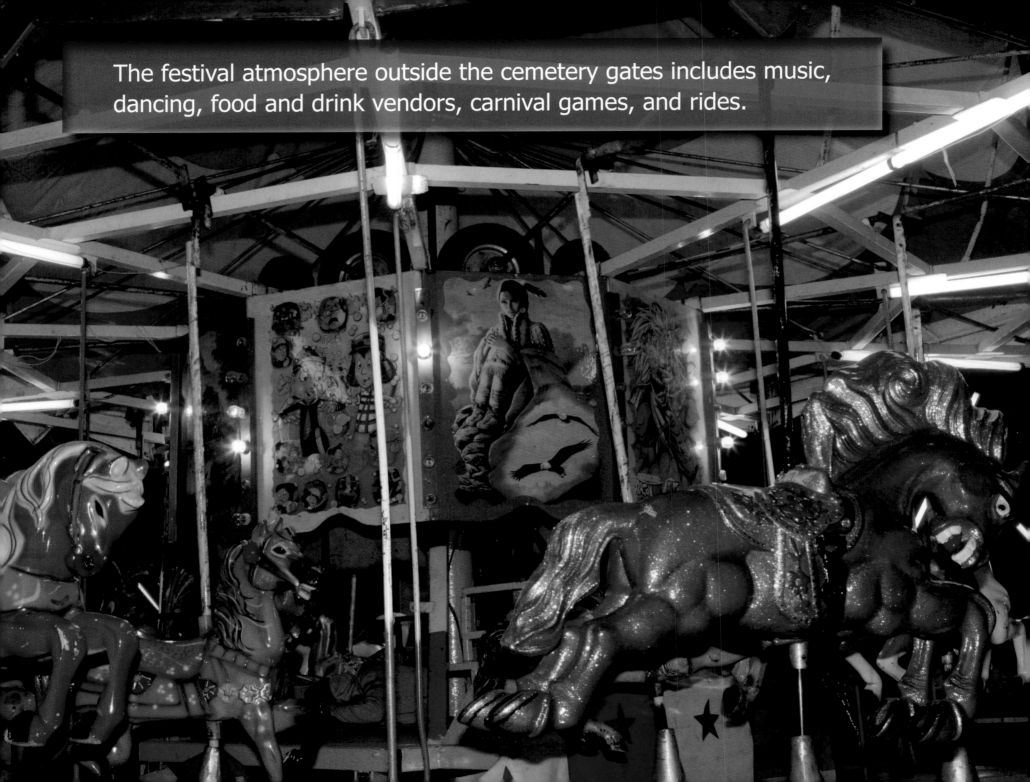

The festival atmosphere outside the cemetery gates includes music, dancing, food and drink vendors, carnival games, and rides.

The comparsa, is generally held after dark, and features merry costumed people, strolling throughout the community. Some *comparsas* are quite large and fill the streets in the center of town. They are often accompanied by loud music and dancing.

Children visit their neighbors in costumes, similar to trick-or-treating in the United States. Instead of receiving candy they are given an *ofrenda* such as bread or fruit from the family's altar.

In some neighborhoods, drums, horns, or even church bells can be heard late into the night as the traveling party wanders the cobblestone streets.

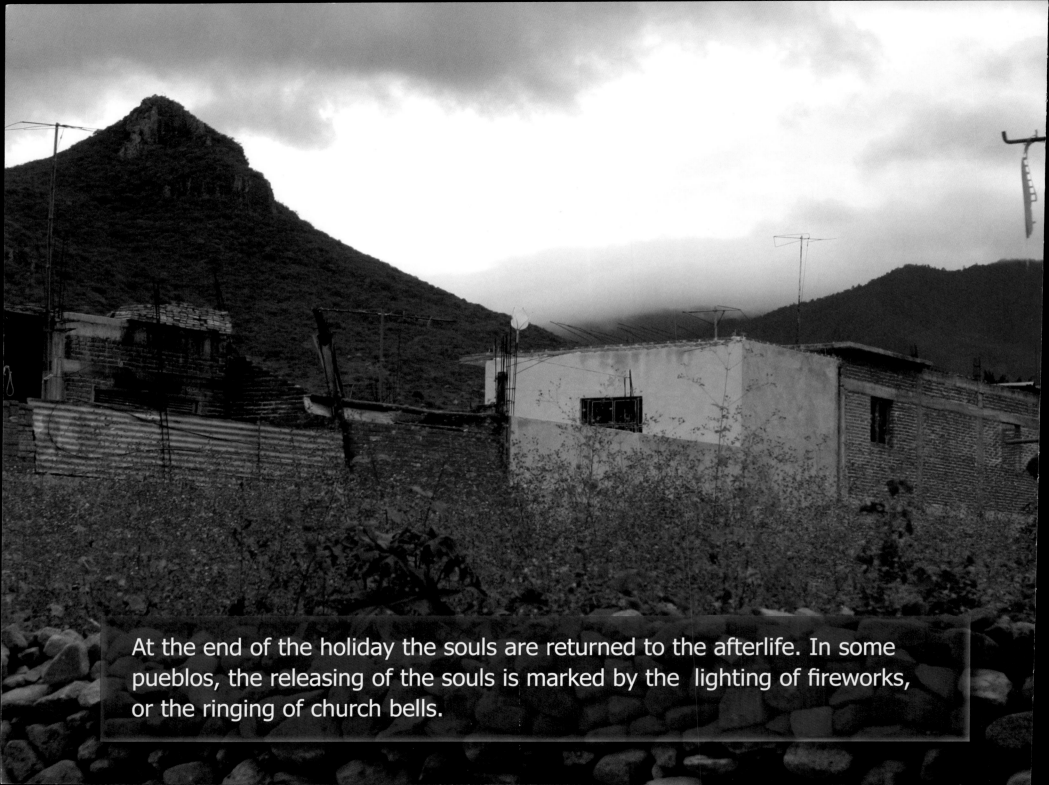

At the end of the holiday the souls are returned to the afterlife. In some pueblos, the releasing of the souls is marked by the lighting of fireworks, or the ringing of church bells.

Over the next few days, altars are taken down, food vendors and carnival games are packed away, and life returns to normal with a renewed sense of family and tradition.

Glossary

Altar de los muertos - offering that family and/or friends prepare for their dead loved ones.

Calacas - whimsical skeleton figures that represent death

Calaveritas de azucar - sugar skulls made for the Dia de los Muertos

Cempazuchitl - yellow marigold, the symbol of death

Copal - scented resin used as incense

Comparsa - parade of dancers and musicians

Dia de los Muertos - Day of the Dead

Fiesta - feast or celebration

Mole - thick sauce made from a variety of ingredients, including chilis, herbs, and spices

Ofrenda - offering; refers to the goods set on the altars

Pan de los muertos - bread made for Day of the Dead meals

Papel picado - colorful tissue paper with intricate, festive designs cut out

Zocolo - center of town

Discussion Questions

1. What similarities do you see between Halloween and Day of the Dead?
2. What differences do you see between Halloween and Day of the Dead?
3. How would you decorate an altar for your family?
4. What are some special foods that you look forward to at holiday time?

Day of the Dead Activities

Build Your Own Altar

Build your altar on a table using boxes to create tiers. Cover with tablecloths. Add photographs of those you are honoring. Decorate with papel picado, calacas, candles, and flowers. Add ofrendas such as calaveras de azucar, pan de muerto, chocolate, and favorite foods.

Papel Picado (Paper Flags)

Using colorful tissue paper, cut shapes and patterns into the flag shaped paper. These paper flags may be used to decorate the altar, or strung together and hung.

Calacas (Whimsical Skeleton Figures)

Using a molding clay of your choice and wire, make skeleton figures.

Tin Lantern Mexican Style

Fill an empty tin can (a soup can will do), with water and put it in freezer until the water is frozen. Place can on a towel and pound nail holes into it to make designs (dots, snowflakes etc.). Let ice melt. If desired, paint with acrylic paint or decorate with permanent markers. Put small candle inside.

Calaveras de Azucar (Sugar Skulls)

1 pound powdered sugar
3 egg whites (lightly beaten)

Combine the sugar and egg whites until they make a semi-firm paste. Mold the paste into skulls. Let dry for 24 hours. Decorate with sprinkles, candies, and icing.

Paper Flowers

Take four to five sheets of 8 inch square tissue paper. Keeping the sheets layered, fold the papers like an accordian so it looks like a thin rectangle. At the center of the rectangle, cut a small v-shaped notch on both sides. Take the end of a pipe cleaner and twist it around the notch. With the stem pointing straight down, gently pull up the layers of paper, one by one. Once all the layers are pulled up, fluff them in place to look natural.